# The
# Puddleman

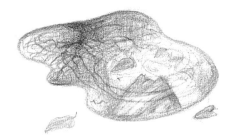

## ALSO BY RAYMOND BRIGGS:

# The
# Puddleman

## RAYMOND BRIGGS

RED FOX

# For
## CONNIE MATILDA & MILES

THE PUDDLEMAN
A RED FOX BOOK 978 0 099 45642 1 (from January 2007)
0 099 45642 7

First published in Great Britain by Jonathan Cape,
an imprint of Random House Children's Books

Jonathan Cape edition published 2004
Red Fox edition published 2006

1 3 5 7 9 10 8 6 4 2

Red Fox Books are published by Random House Children's Books,
61–63 Uxbridge Road, London W5 5SA,
a division of The Random House Group Ltd,
in Australia by Random House Australia (Pty) Ltd,
20 Alfred Street, Milsons Point, Sydney, NSW 2061, Australia,
in New Zealand by Random House New Zealand Ltd,
18 Poland Road, Glenfield, Auckland 10, New Zealand,
and in South Africa by Random House (Pty) Ltd, Isle of Houghton,
Corner Boundary Road & Carse O'Gowrie, Houghton 2198, South Africa

THE RANDOM HOUSE GROUP Limited Reg. No. 954009
www.kidsatrandomhouse.co.uk

A CIP catalogue record for this book is available from the British Library.

Printed in Singapore

We've all gone away.

Would you like to give me a hand?

Yes, but I've got Collar
on a lead.

Is that your dog?

No.
It's my grandfather.

Oh, an old boy like that
can look after himself.

Are they puddles
on your back?

Yes, that's right.
There's all different sizes
of puddles nowadays.
They have to fit the hollows
in the ground, see?

Have you got the
big, yellowy one?

Oh, yes. I know the one you mean.
If you like, we'll do that one first.
I'll be pleased to be rid of it.
It's far and away the heaviest one.

Look, now here's a pretty one. You can see the sky in it. Is this Connie?

Connie does ballet. She's long and thin. It might be her.

And maybe this one is Tilly? It's got clouds and flying birds. Let's try it in the hollow.

Yes! It fits! It's Connie!

Tilly is strong. She hugs me. Sometimes she sits on me.

It goes in! It's Tilly!

But ...
where did you get
the water from?

It's not WATER, silly!
It's PUDDLES!

Yes, but I don't see how—

The Puddle Man
GAVE them to me!

Oh, you mean a farmer
with a water tank
on the back of his tractor?

NO! Silly!
The Puddle Man had them
on his back.

Had the puddles
ON HIS BACK!

YES! I helped him.
We put them in.
They were warm.

So they went home to Grannie's house for a tea of beans on toast with black and trees.

THE END

With grateful acknowledgements
to MILES for
The naming of puddles
Collar
I think...I THINK this one...MIGHT be Auntie Clare
Black
They haven't put any puddle in that one
Trees
Silly!